Miss Janie's
Class!

Keep your star
in view!

Sydney's Star

Enjoy!

Peter H. Reynolds

For Sarah, my own inventive, creative star.
Keep shining!
Love, Dad

SIMON & SCHUSTER BOOKS FOR YOUNG READERS
An imprint of Simon & Schuster Children's Publishing Division
1230 Avenue of the Americas, New York, New York 10020

Book design by Anahid Hamparian and Peter H. Reynolds
The text of this book is set in Classical Garamond.
The illustrations are rendered with brush, watercolor, gouache, and tea.

Printed in Hong Kong
2 4 6 8 10 9 7 5 3 1
Library of Congress Cataloging-in-Publication Data
Reynolds, Peter.
Sydney's star / written and illustrated by Peter H. Reynolds.— 1st ed.
p. cm.
Summary: The malfunction of Sydney's mechanical star leads her to an unexpected happy ending.
ISBN 0-689-83184-6
[1. Inventors—Fiction. 2. Stars—Fiction.] I. Title.
PZ7.R337645 Sy 2001
[E]—dc21
00-045064

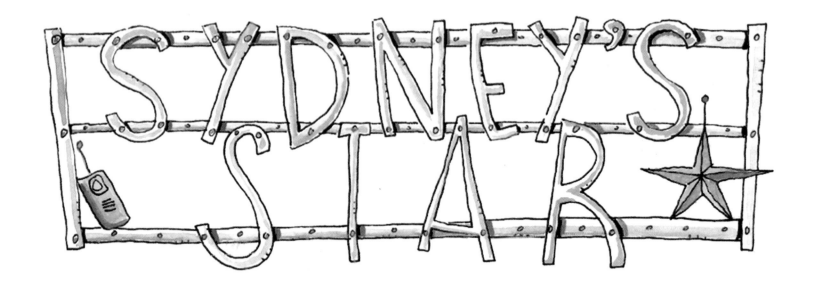

SYDNEY'S STAR

Written & illustrated by

Peter H. Reynolds

Simon & Schuster Books for Young Readers

New York   London   Toronto   Sydney   Singapore

$\mathcal{S}$ydney loved to build things. She made brilliant birdhouses, charming cheesecakes, and all sorts of wonderful inventions.

Sydney was inspired by the world around her.

One night a bright star caught her attention. It sparkled gold and silver. Sydney wished she could just reach out and touch it, but she knew it was millions of miles away.

"A star! That's it! I'll build a remote-control star!"

She made lots of sketches and miniature models. When her plans were done she went to work.

She tested, fine-tuned, fiddled, and tweaked until at last she was done.

Standing back, Sydney pressed the remote control.

The star flew up! It glowed and spun and sparkled in the twilight sky.

Sydney decided to take her star to the Student Science Fair. She hoped she'd win. The lucky winner would receive a blue ribbon *and* a beautiful telescope.

Sydney waited to share her creation.

One boy showed a clock that was powered by a potato.
The crowd cheered. Sydney was impressed too.

A girl wowed the crowd with her bubble-making
bicycle. The crowd ooohed and aaahed, and so did Sydney.

Finally it was Sydney's turn.
She took a deep breath and pushed her wagon onto center stage. The wheels squeaked loudly as the crowd slowly went silent.

She stood tall and explained her invention and what it could do.

Everyone in the crowd held their breath as Sydney pressed go. The star rose up—it spun and bounced. It flashed colors. It beamed like a lighthouse.

Everyone cheered!

Sydney smiled ear to ear and bowed her best bow.

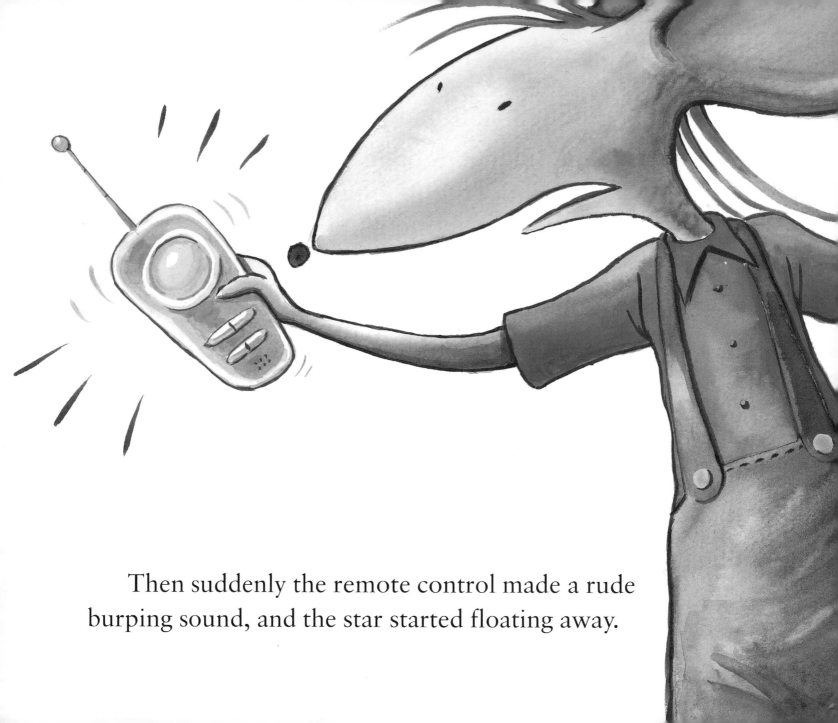

Then suddenly the remote control made a rude
burping sound, and the star started floating away.

Sydney yelled for the star to come back, but it was no use. The crowd began to laugh, then slowly went quiet.

Sydney turned four shades of red as she sadly watched her star drift away.

She left the Student Science Fair having lost the contest
and her star.

She walked home along the beach. It was becoming foggy
and dark. She walked faster. It started to rain.

At the same time somewhere out at sea, a boat struggled
to find the shore and avoid the rocks. Captain Stilton was
delighted to see the glow of a lighthouse in the distance. But
was it a lighthouse? She rubbed her eyes and looked again.

It was a star! A floating star. A flashing, floating, mechanical star! Captain Stilton was amazed to see a star flashing a message in Morse code!

The message said, "Picked up a distress signal. Came to help."

Back on the dock near her house, Sydney pondered in the rain. "Where could my star be?" As she gazed out into the misty ocean, she saw a glow—a flashing. It grew bigger and clearer. Sydney couldn't believe her eyes! Floating near the shore was her star.

And right behind it was a boat being safely guided to the dock.

"Is that *your* star?" the captain asked when Sydney had finished jumping up and down with joy.

"Yes, I made it!" she squealed. Sydney and the captain chatted back and forth as Sydney led the way to her family's house. Her star followed.

Sydney's family invited the captain to stay for dinner. Afterward the captain thanked Sydney's parents; then she turned to Sydney and said, "I'll be in touch." It had been an amazing day, Sydney was sure of that. So before she went to bed she leaned out her window and looked up . . .

and Sydney's star signaled a colorful,
bright, starry good night.